The Cat

Written by Jane Hileman & Marilyn Pitt

Illustrated by John Bianchi

Come, dog.

Come see what I have.

This is cat.
This is a little cat.

She will live with us.
She will live here.

Do you like the cat?

I like the cat.

Look, she likes your bed.

Look, she likes your food.

Look, she likes you.